This book belongs to

....

Quarto Knows

Quarto is the authority on a wide range of topics.

Quarto educates, entertains and enriches the lives of our readers—enthusiasts and lovers of hands-on living.

www.quartoknows.com

© 2018 Quarto Publishing plc

First published in 2018 by QED Publishing, an imprint of The Quarto Group.
The Old Brewery, 6 Blundell Street,
London N7 9BH, United Kingdom.
T (0)20 7700 6700 F (0)20 7700 8066
www.QuartoKnows.com

A catalogue record for this book is available from the British Library.

ISBN 978-1-78493-921-2

Based on the original story by Kate Petty and Maribel Suarez
Author of adapted text: Katie Woolley
Series Editor: Joyce Bentley
Series Designer: Sarah Peden

Manufactured in Dongguan, China TL102017

9 8 7 6 5 4 3 2 1

MIX
Paper from responsible sources
FSC® C104723
FSC www.fsc.org

Reading Gems

Gus

at Big School

QED

Flora and Dora
went to big school.

Gus was too little.
He had to stay
at home.

Gus played with
his toys.

Flora and Dora played
with Gus after school.

The next day Flora and Dora
went to school again.

Gus was sad.

Dora and Flora go to school
with dad the next day too.

Mum, when can I go to big school?

Gus stayed at home again.

He was sad.

At last Gus could go to school!

I am at big school.

23

Story Words

Dad

Dora

Flora

Gus

home

Mum

school

toys

Let's Talk About Gus at Big School

Look at the book cover.

What do you think Gus is doing in the picture?

What toys can you see?

Do you have a favourite toy?

Gus is pretending to be a teacher on pages 6 and 7.

Why do you think he is playing 'schools'?

What dressing up games do you like to play at home?

Gus has two big sisters called Dora and Flora.

What initial letter sound does each name begin with?

Can you think of any other words that begin with the same initial letter sounds?

Talk about your school day.

What do you do in the morning before school?

How do you get to school?

What do you like best about school?

Talk about the end of the story.

Did you like the ending?

Do you think Gus is happy or sad?

Fun and Games

Can you finish these sentences with the correct word?

Can I go to big .... ?

school | play | Mum

You are too ....

little | big | school

Gus played with his ....

toys | Mum | big

Answers: school, little, toys.

Can you play 'I Spy' with Gus? Find a picture of a word that begins with each of these letters.

G   T   M   S

Your Turn

Now that you have read the story,
have a go at telling it in your own words.
Use the pictures below to help you.

31

GET TO KNOW READING GEMS

Reading Gems is a series of books that has been written for children who are learning to read. The books have been created in consultation with a literacy specialist.

The books fit into four levels, with each level getting more challenging as a child's confidence and reading ability grows. The simple text and fun illustrations provide gradual, structured practice of reading. Most importantly, these books are good stories that are fun to read!

Level 1 is for children who are taking their first steps into reading. Story themes and subjects are familiar to young children, and there is lots of repetition to build reading confidence.

Level 2 is for children who have taken their first reading steps and are becoming readers. Story themes are still familiar but sentences are a bit longer, as children begin to tackle more challenging vocabulary.

Level 3 is for children who are developing as readers. Stories and subjects are varied, and more descriptive words are introduced.

Level 4 is for readers who are rapidly growing in reading confidence and independence. There is less repetition on the page, broader themes are explored and plot lines straddle multiple pages.

Gus at Big School follows a little boy who is desperate to start school. It explores themes of growing up, school and play.

Level 1

Gus stayed at home again.
He was sad.

Short sentences ✓

Simple vocabulary ✓

Lots of repetition ✓

Pictures and words support one another ✓